TQB

MAR 0 9 2006

 W9-BAI-559

E HAYLES
Hayles, Marsha.
Pajamas anytime /

PALM BEACH COUNTY
LIBRARY SYSTEM
3650 SUMMIT BLVD.
WEST PALM BEACH, FLORIDA 33406

Pajamas Anytime

Marsha Hayles

ILLUSTRATED BY

Hiroe Nakata

G. P. PUTNAM'S SONS · NEW YORK

Text copyright © 2005 by Marsha Hayles.
Illustrations copyright © 2005 by Hiroe Nakata.
All rights reserved. This book, or parts thereof, may not be
reproduced in any form without permission in writing
from the publisher, G. P. Putnam's Sons, a division of
Penguin Young Readers Group, 345 Hudson Street, New
York, NY 10014. G. P. Putnam's Sons, Reg. U.S. Pat. & Tm.
Off. The scanning, uploading and distribution of this book via the
Internet or via any other means without the permission of the
publisher is illegal and punishable by law. Please purchase only
authorized electronic editions, and do not participate in or encourage
electronic piracy of copyrighted materials. Your support of the
author's rights is appreciated. Published simultaneously in
Canada. Manufactured in China by South China Printing Co.
Ltd. Designed by Marikka Tamura. Text set in Oliver.
The art was done in watercolor and gouache.
Library of Congress Cataloging-in-Publication Data
Hayles, Marsha. Pajamas anytime / Marsha Hayles;
illustrated by Hiroe Nakata. p. cm. Summary:
Each month of the year presents a special
occasion when pajamas are the perfect thing to
wear. (1. Pajamas—Fiction. 2. Months—Fiction. 3. Stories in
rhyme.) I. Nakata, Hiroe, ill. II. Title. PZ8.3.H326 Paj 2005
(E)—dc21 2002006355 ISBN 0-399-23871-9
10 9 8 7 6 5 4 3 2 1
First Impression

To all the Watson cousins who bunked in with me,
and especially in memory of Steve. —M. H.

To A. Y. —H. N.

If January's snow
Closes school for the day

Or my February cold
Keeps me sofa'd from play

Time for pajamas, my jamas,

mine-o

During March family night
Playing board games inside

Or puddle-splash April
When I'm tumble-towel dried

Time for pajamas,

my jamas, mine-o

For Mother's Day May
Making pancakes in stacks

Or a June night away
When I ride Grandpa's back

Time for pajamas,

my jamas, mine-o

On the Fourth of July
When the sky glitter glows

Or a hot August night
When my belly button shows

Time for pajamas,

my jamas, mine-o

When our September school party
Has us all dressed for bed

Or in pumpkin October
When ghost stories are read

Time for pajamas,

my jamas, mine-o

For Thanksgiving November
Cousins bunk in with me

Then out goes December
In a confetti-snow spree!

Time for pajamas,

my jamas, mine-o

A year of pajamas
Like a soft lullaby

Helps sleep come along

Till my mind fills with sky

Time for **pajamas,**

my jamas,

Night-o . . .